ISAIAH TREE

ISBN 978-1-68526-014-9 (Paperback)
ISBN 978-1-68526-015-6 (Digital)

Covenant Books
11661 Hwy 707
Murrells Inlet, SC 29576
www.covenantbooks.com

ISAIAH TREE

Anna Lea Cannon

Illustrated by Leisha Black

The young olive tree nearly burst with joy as it saw the new words Isaiah wrote as he sat in the shade of its branches.

"For unto us a child is born, unto us a son is given: and his name shall be called Wonderful Counselor, The Mighty God, The Everlasting Father, The Prince of Peace" (Isa. 9:6).

Isaiah frequently came to write under the young tree who loved to glance down and read his words. Other trees in the orchard called the young tree Isaiah Tree because it always passed on the interesting words of the poet. But these were the most exciting words yet.

Could this child Isaiah wrote about be the one that its parent tree had talked about and that all the other olive trees told stories about? Could this child that was coming have taken part in creation itself? Isaiah Tree shivered with joy, thinking of the possibility of seeing this newborn babe. Maybe his crib would be made from its branches. Isaiah Tree excitedly passed on rustling whispers of Isaiah's words in the olive grove. "The Prince, the Prince, the Prince of Peace is coming."

This swishing murmur grew louder as all the trees awoke with excitement. They proudly retold the story of the olive tree's importance to the earth. They all knew that a dove had plucked off an olive branch many years earlier to let Noah's family know the floodwaters had finally receded. Each tree since then held its branches higher and more nobly when they told the story to younger trees. This olive branch meant Noah's family could get off the ark and live with each other in peace.

Since then, "extending an olive branch" has been a symbol of peace.

Olive trees knew that when they got very old and no longer produced an abundant crop of olives, the farmer would cut them down. However, the farmer would leave new shoots coming from the base of the tree. When this new tree grew, the farmer would then graft in branches from other high-producing trees. Thus, one tree never really died, but rather gave new life to young sprouts.

Old roots, neighboring branches, and new trees were all interconnected as they supported each other and grew.

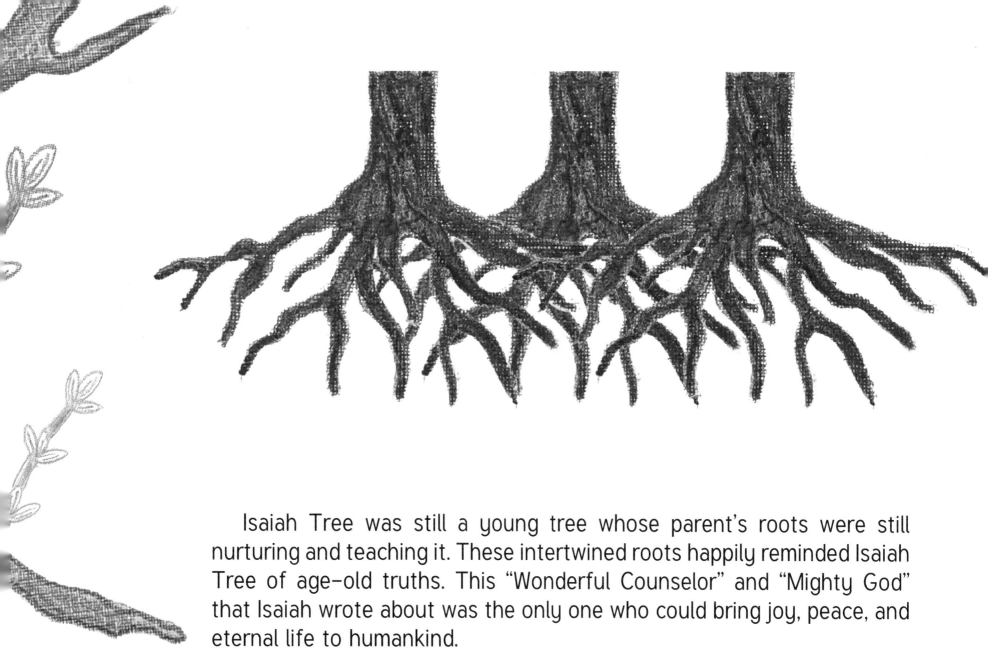

Isaiah Tree was still a young tree whose parent's roots were still nurturing and teaching it. These intertwined roots happily reminded Isaiah Tree of age-old truths. This "Wonderful Counselor" and "Mighty God" that Isaiah wrote about was the only one who could bring joy, peace, and eternal life to humankind.

Isaiah Tree knew that it would always be part of new generations of trees. However, it still longed to see and know "The Prince of Peace" with all its present limbs, trunk, and leaves before being cut down.

Isaiah Tree loved to read its namesake's other words as Isaiah wrote and pondered, sitting on a low-lying branch.

"And there shall come forth a rod out of the stem of Jesse and a branch shall grow out of his roots" (Isaiah 11: 1–2).

Isaiah Tree was proud of its inherent ability to rejuvenate that could allow it to be used for such a beautiful metaphor. It also was proud of the fact that humans were so dependent on the olive for oil and fruit.

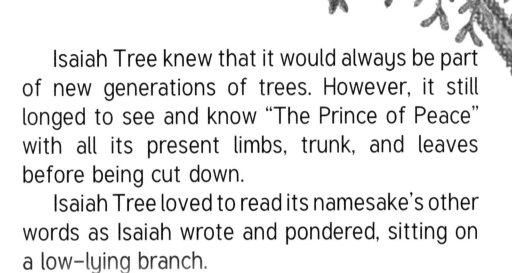

Isaiah Tree had heard a discussion between Isaiah and his friend that Moses had commanded that "pure olive oil beaten for the light" would cause the tabernacle's light to always burn. (Exodus 27:20).

Could Isaiah Tree somehow pass on that light from the Prince of Peace to the world?

Soon after the joyful rustling caused by Isaiah's words, Isaiah Tree got to participate in an additional way olive trees propagate. A farmer came and chose several of its healthy branches, scored them with a knife, peeled back some bark, and wrapped a small handful of soil and some cloth around the spot.

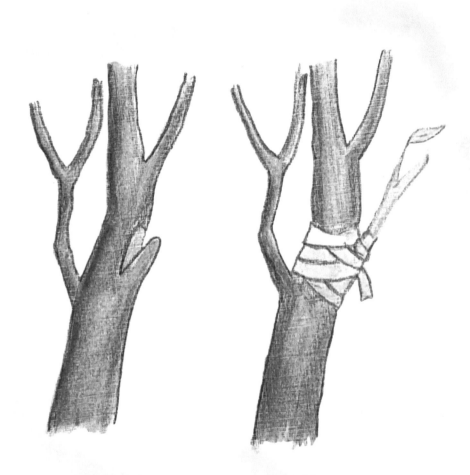

It hurt a little; but Isaiah Tree knew that soon roots would grow where the peeled-off bark had been. Then the farmer would cut the branches and plant the new baby trees in new places.

Isaiah Tree whispered to the small branches as they were leaving that as they grew, they should send messages back as small twigs carried by doves if something exciting happened in their lives.

Isaiah hadn't come to write in the olive grove for many years, and other changes had happened as well. Most trees that were Isaiah Tree's peers had been cut down, and their shoots were now mature trees—only a couple of Isaiah Tree's original friends were still standing.

These elderly trees talked about how fortunate they were that families frequently came to have picnics under them. They liked having the children climb up their trunks and swing from their branches. They were also excited to hear the picnickers talking about how it was so remarkable to have trees that were over five hundred years old still growing. These picnickers thought the owners of this garden called Gethsemane planned to let the trees grow as long as they could.

Isaiah Tree's heart swelled with hope. Perhaps it would still live long enough to see this amazing Prince of Peace come to the world.

Then, about seven hundred years from when Isaiah Tree first sprouted, a dove brought a message from one of Isaiah Tree's elderly children in Bethlehem. There were strange things happening! A baby had been born. Shepherds had come to kneel at a manger where the baby lay, and a new star was shining directly down on the babe. Isaiah Tree looked up; there was an amazing new star. What did it mean? Could this be the child?

A few years later, a dove brought back a twig from a tree by the temple. A twelve-year-old boy had confounded the wise men in the temple.

Then eighteen years later, another dove brought back tales of an amazing sermon given on a small mountain by the babe now grown to manhood.

This grown-up babe healed the sick, miraculously fed multitudes, and calmed the sea. Fishermen had left their nets to become his disciples.

The old tree's roots and branches quivered with joy. Had the Prince of Peace Isaiah wrote about finally come? Had Isaiah Tree lived long enough to have this man walk in his garden? He hoped so. But what would compel the Prince of Peace to come to this garden?

Then one evening, way past the time families usually came to picnic in the garden, Isaiah Tree noticed a man approaching, followed by eleven others. The man paused, and three continued on with him. He asked those three to please watch while he went to pray.

Then, he went about a stone's throw away from them right to Isaiah Tree. He knelt down by the old tree and tenderly touched and blessed Isaiah Tree. He thanked the tree for supporting him. Then he began praying in earnest, "Father, if thou be willing, remove this cup from me: nevertheless, not my will, but thine, be done" (Luke 22:42).

Though the man seemed weighed down with grief, he was filled with power and light. Compassionately, an angel appeared from heaven to strengthen him.

The tree trembled with joy to the tips of its branches and roots thinking about Isaiah's words about the coming Messiah. This had to be the Prince of Peace Isaiah wrote about.

After the angel left, his followers fell into a deep slumber. This Wonderful Counselor then seemed profoundly, deeply alone as he uttered a prayer incomprehensible to mere mortals. He prayed for the men who had come with him who were in an exhausted sleep. He asked that they would be strengthened in the coming hours of certain terror.

But his prayer didn't stop there. It grew out like the ancient supporting roots of Isaiah Tree to encompass the whole of humanity. He prayed for his Father to forgive the wrongs others had done to each other and themselves since the beginning of time and until the end of the world. He begged that each would see and know the Father's love for them individually so they could use that knowledge to spread peace and love throughout the world.

Incredibly, this amazing peacemaker seemed to know the names and feelings of all men who would ever or had ever lived on the earth. Not only did he know them, but he also willingly suffered all their pains.

The joy the tree had felt turned to despair as a portion of the weight of agony passed into its very being. How could this Prince of Peace bear this incomprehensible suffering, and why was he bearing this unendurable pain all alone? Would this suffering be like the olive oil in the tabernacle lamps that would keep giving peace and light to the world forever and stop the power of darkness?

Suddenly, the tree felt teardrops on its trunk and then, to its horror, something much heavier than tears. Drops of blood were dripping onto the tree branch where he knelt. The drops spotted the branch and then fell to the ground as this king suffered and prayed not for himself but for all men. Though he was royal and regal in his suffering, the tree didn't know how this Savior could continue on and stay alive with this extreme physical pain.

22

A tumultuous noise interrupted the Messiah's pleading as a great multitude entered with lanterns, torches, and weapons. The Prince of Peace arose. The one leading the soldiers came and gave a traitorous kiss to the suffering prince who was soaked with blood. This great prince asked them who they were looking for. They answered, "Jesus of Nazareth." The prince replied, "I am he." The soldiers were so surprised at Jesus's nobility that they fell backwards, and Jesus had to ask again whom they sought. When they asked him again, he responded, "I have told you that I am he: if therefore ye seek me, let these go their way" (John 18:7).

24

One of the previously slumbering men then jumped up and sliced off the ear of one who came to capture the man they called Jesus. At this, Jesus, amidst the great confusion and fear of his apostles, picked up the ear and put it back on, healing one of his enemies. The Prince of Peace could show kindness even in a tumult of fear.

Isaiah Tree had never seen such love amidst hate. This love continued as The Prince stepped back and placed his hands on the tree as if resting, but the tree heard an unspoken blessing.

"Isaiah Tree, your wishful prayers have been answered. Your limbs and branches have lived to see me. Now, your progeny will live in this very garden until the end of time to bear witness to the world that I died. Countless visitors the world over will come to this garden to be reminded that life goes on even past the thousand years an olive tree can live. Though I will be crucified, in three days, I will rise again. Because of that and the suffering I bore by this tree, all can be forgiven through belief on my name. They can live forever, for you have seen the Prince of Peace."

The tumultuous crowd hurried him away. There was a hushed silence in the olive orchard, for all had seen the suffering yet unspeakable majesty of the prophesied Messiah.

When Isaiah Tree's life was finally over, a new branch grew out of its roots. As Isaiah Tree's roots encircled its offspring, it whispered that the world was no longer waiting for the Prince of Peace. He had come! His blood had created fertile soil for all who would believe on his name. He lived again and had conquered death through the suffering he had endured in the Garden of Gethsemane and on the cross.

If one walks quietly under those ancient olive trees, they can still hear and rejoice in the olive trees' whisperings that Christ's love can bring peace and light to the world. Isaiah Tree's posterity still knows that the symbol of their light glowing in the temple represents the majestic love and light from the Savior that will glow forever.

About the Illustrator

Leisha Black has a love for art and children and children's literature.

She began exploring drawing and painting at a young age while on family camping trips, painting outdoor scenes with a box of watercolors. Watercolor has become her favorite medium. While majoring in elementary education, she specialized in Fine Arts and Children's Literature. While teaching fifth and sixth grades, she completed a master's degree in library and information sciences with the aim of becoming an elementary school librarian.

After only a few years, she left teaching to raise her six children. It wasn't long before she was involved as a volunteer coordinator of parents, teaching art to the elementary classes in her neighborhood school. When that school was converted to a charter school, she helped to establish weekly specialty classes of art history and elements of art as part of the curriculum. She has been the art specialist now at Canyon Rim Elementary for fifteen years, teaching art to first, third, and fifth graders. She also directs a Shakespearean play every year at the school, including making many of the costumes.

About the Author

A few years ago, Anna Lea traveled to Jerusalem. One of the highlights of the trip was standing in the Garden of Gethsemane and thinking about how Jesus Christ willingly suffered to pay the price for her mistakes and the mistakes of the whole world. Jesus Christ sweat great drops of blood to ensure that all could receive forgiveness for their sins. She thought about how this sacrifice was all-encompassing yet, at the same time, was individual enough to include her husband, five children, their spouses, and five grandchildren.

She was intrigued with how old the olive trees were with their gnarled trunks and branches. Upon researching, she found that these trees regenerate with sprouts in a way that links them to one another through antiquity. This eternal nature is very symbolic as it relates to Christ and his power to bring all of God's children eternal life.

The intergenerational linkage of olive trees resembles the intergenerational ties of families. This appeals to Anna Lea, who comes from a family of nine children—two girls and seven boys. Her parents now have a posterity of over 140, so being connected like the olive trees are connected as a family is deeply meaningful to her.

Anna Lea is an elementary school teacher and loves working with children. She especially enjoys teaching science because it allows children to discover the wonders of God's creations in the rocks, flowers, butterflies, and plants. She likes gardening, canning, stained glass, discovering fun children's literature, singing, writing music, hiking, and serving as a volunteer in her church.

CPSIA information can be obtained
at www.ICGtesting.com
Printed in the USA
BVHW060057200922
647446BV00001B/1